For Jessica
M.G.
For my son Luke,
Jill and my godchildren
H.D.L.

First edition for the United States and Canada
published 1992 by Barron's Educational Series, Inc.

Originally published by J.M. Dent & Sons Ltd,
91 Clapham High Street, London SW4 7TA.

The title in the United Kingdom is *Rosie's Lion*.

Text first published in *The Lost Ones* under the title
"Beyond the Door," copyright © Margaret Greaves, 1991.
Text changes for this edition copyright ©
Margaret Greaves, 1992.
Illustrations copyright © Honey de Lacey, 1992.

All inquiries should be addressed to:
Barron's Educational Series, Inc.
250 Wireless Boulevard
Hauppauge, New York 11788

Library of Congress Catalog Card No. 92-951

International Standard Book No. 0-8120-6279-5

Library of Congress Cataloging-in-Publication Data

Greaves, Margaret.
    Sarah's lion/by Margaret Greaves; illustrated by
Honey De Lacey. —First ed.
         p.   cm.
    Summary: Sarah, a young princess whose desire
to explore is thwarted by her family because it is not
appropriate for her position, eventually goes off alone
with a friendly lion.
    ISBN 0-8120-6279-5
    [1. Princesses—Fiction.   2. Behavior—Fiction.
3. Lions—Fiction.]   I. De Lacey, Honey, ill.   II. Title.
PZ7.G8Ro 1992   92-951
[E]—dc20   CIP
                                                        AC

PRINTED IN ITALY
2345   987654321

SARAH'S LION

Margaret Greaves

Illustrated by

Honey de Lacey

BARRON'S

Sarah, the small princess, was much younger than her sisters. When they were nearly grown up she still had lessons with her governess, and very dull they were. When they walked in the palace gardens, Sarah sometimes saw glimpses of wild woods and fields beyond the palace gates, but when she asked to walk there her governess became annoyed.

"They are not safe," she said sharply, "and they would make your dress dirty. You should be happy to walk here in your own beautiful garden."

Sarah thought the garden would be more beautiful if even one of the paths had a curve in it or a single tulip grew out of place. But she never said so.

She was happiest in her own bedroom at the top of the east tower, where sometimes she could be alone. It had three windows. From one she could see a great stretch of forest where trees tossed in the wind and little ragged bushes grew freely below them and the wild birds flew up in flocks. The second window looked toward a long range of mountains, so far away that they were sometimes no more than a blue shadow against the sky.

From the third window she saw the town spreading downward from the palace to the farms and fields and gentle countryside. Beyond that, a glittering blue ribbon on sunshiny days, a misty gray one on cloudy days, and nothing but pale mist on rainy days, was the sea. The small princess had never been near the sea, but she thought it the most wonderful mystery of all. It had no barriers except the sky itself.

"Sarah," said the Queen one day, "you are more grown up now. What would you like to do?"

"Oh, *please!*" cried Sarah. "I should like to ride to the mountains and climb to the very top and see what is on the other side."

"Are you mad?" demanded the Queen.

"No princess would dream of such behavior!" said her eldest sister.

"Who knows what dangers may be there?" protested the second. "Goblins, or dragons, or ghosts!"

"Stupid child," scolded the third. "When *will* you learn to be a proper princess?"

The Queen ordered shutters to close the window that looked toward the mountains.

Sarah went sadly to her own room that night. She opened the door, then closed it quickly again with a little cry of fright and fled back down the stairs. The third princess was just then walking by.

"Whatever is the matter?" she asked.

"There's a lion in my room," chattered Sarah. "A great big golden lion."

"Nonsense," said her sister. "How could there be a lion in your room? Don't make up silly stories."

She walked on, and Sarah slowly climbed the stairs again. Perhaps she had only imagined the lion.

She opened her door carefully, and there he still was—very beautiful, golden as sand, with great golden eyes. He touched her hand gently with his nose, padded to the shuttered window and tore a great scratch down the wood, then turned to the door as if he wanted her to follow.

"No," said the small princess. "They would be afraid of you down there. They would kill you."

All that evening she sat beside the golden lion and stroked his fur and talked to him, and at last fell asleep with her head against his flank. In the morning she woke in her own bed and the lion had gone.

Now Sarah watched the distant mountains more than ever, and longed to run on their slopes and feel the wind in her hair.

At long last she grew old enough to leave the palace schoolroom and join the older princesses.

"Now," said the Queen, "you are nearly grown up. What would you like to do?"

"Oh, please," said Sarah joyfully, "may I walk in the forest beyond the palace gates?"

"*What?*" cried the Queen, shocked.

"No princess walks in a wild wood," said the first princess.

"It would not be safe," shuddered the second.

"Only a silly child would think of such a thing," said the third princess scornfully.

The Queen gave orders that shutters should be put up over the window that looked toward the forest.

Very sadly the small princess went to her room that night. The lion was waiting for her. He looked thinner, his golden hide seemed dull, and he paced to and fro as if the room were a cage. She threw her arms around his neck, and his purr rumbled like distant thunder. Then he shook her off and padded to the door as if to get out.

"No, no," said the small princess. "I'm sure they would kill you down there."

At that he lay down beside her, and their sadness flowed into each other until they found some comfort and fell asleep. But in the morning Sarah woke in her own bed and the lion had gone.

After another while the Queen said, "Surely you are now grown up. What would you like to do?"

"I don't know," said Sarah. "What do proper princesses do?"

"Nothing, of course," said the first princess.

"But we do it very elegantly," said the second.

"And we spend much time being beautiful," said the third.

"Oh, dear!" said the small princess sadly. "I don't know how to do nothing. And I shall never, never be beautiful."

She was quite right. All her sisters were tall and slim, with yellow hair and violet-blue eyes. Sarah was short and plump, with tawny-brown hair. Her eyes were flecked with gold.

Sadly she went back to her own room. The lion was there. He was even thinner than before. His sand-gold fur was rubbed as if against the bars of a cage. When he saw the small princess he dropped his head on her feet, and golden tears ran from his golden eyes and down his beautiful broad golden nose. Sarah's own tears fell into his mane.

"Wait!" she said at last. "Wait. Don't leave me tonight. Let us wait until the palace is asleep."

A long time they waited, until at last the Queen and the three princesses and the servants went to bed. The small princess opened her door and listened.

"Come," she murmured, laying her hand on the lion's head.

Together they slipped through the open door and went lightly down the stairs. A curtain whispered in the darkness, falling ash settled softly in the dying fire. But the drowsy guards never saw or heard them as they passed.

A dog barked in the courtyard but no one noticed. The gates of the palace garden swung open to let them through. Side by side, golden under the rising moon, they slipped through the edge of the forest and on toward the limitless sea.

"Whatever can have happened to Sarah?" said the Queen the next day.

"She's run away," said the first princess.

"Just as well," said the second. "She would never have made a proper princess."

"She *said* there was a lion in her room," mused the third. "Perhaps it has eaten her up."

But of course she was wrong.

For many years after that, there were strange reports from travelers abroad at night. Some had caught sight of a girl and a great beast wandering side by side through the forest. Others had glimpsed them against the skyline of a mountain.

Strangest of all, some said they had seen them dancing with their own black shadows on the white and moonlit sands beside the sea. But as the Queen and the three elder princesses never went beyond the palace gardens, they never heard any of the stories.